SUBSPACE

MANDIE MILLS

13 Red Media Ltd.

Subspace

Cover Design by Emily Irwin

Proofreading by The Book Fox

To E.L., for helping me realize it's never too late to live the life you want.

ACKNOWLEDGMENTS

I'd like to thank the team at 13 Red Media, especially Taylor Saracen, for giving me the chance to share my stories.

Subspace
By Mandie Mills

1

My eyes scanned the room as I lifted my beer to my lips. It figured Trey would bail on me. He was the one who'd wanted to come to this stupid party, and even though I'd known his "I'll meet you there" was really code for "There's almost no chance I'm going to show up," I'd come anyway.

This wasn't my scene. I wasn't into Greek life. Parties were fun, and I'd never say no to drinking my face off, but the whole fraternity life wasn't for me. I was a nerd. I liked gaming and chilling with my friends. Keg stands and hazing weren't things that interested me in the least.

I'd thought Trey was the same way, but then he'd gone and fallen head over heels in lust with a sorority girl who wouldn't give him the time of day. For one thing, she was a senior and he was a freshman like me, and for another, she was way out of his league. I loved Trey like a brother, but he was even more of a nerd than I was.

"Now, you don't look old enough to be holding that drink."

I heard a smooth and deep voice behind me and shifted my gaze so it landed on the guy who'd spoken.

Holy shit, he was hot. I wasn't a small dude, at five-foot-ten, but this guy had to be at least six-one or six-two. He had that killer combo of dark brown hair and piercing blue eyes that could bring me to my knees every time, and his face was perfection. His tight black t-shirt and jeans framed his toned and tight body, and the bulge in his jeans left nothing to the imagination.

"Are you trying to get me and my brothers in trouble, kid?"

"Kid? That's rich." I turned so we were facing each other. "Hello, teapot, I have a kettle I'd like you to meet."

He let out a throaty laugh and looked me up and down. It wasn't in a I'm-blatantly-checking you-out way. It was in more of an appraising way. Like how you'd check out a pair of shoes you were thinking of buying.

"You don't think I'm twenty-one?" he asked, one eyebrow lifting to give him a cocky look.

"I really don't care either way." I shrugged and tried not to show how much that look affected me. Cocky guys were my kryptonite. I didn't like arrogant, but cocky and confident was so fucking sexy it could make me go from a *hard no* to a *fuck yes* in a heartbeat. "So you're what, the ID police?" I lifted my red solo cup to my lips and took a generous swallow. I didn't know if this dude was straight, gay, bi, or curious, but he'd started it, so I wasn't going to hold back. A little flirting would either tell me he played for my team or send him running. Or get me clocked in the face.

Keeping my eyes on his, I lowered the cup and slowly let my tongue sweep over my bottom lip. The mystery guy didn't flinch or swing. Instead, he let his eyes follow my tongue as he wet his own full lips in a move that looked almost compulsive.

So, he was at least on the curious side of the spectrum. Good to know.

"Just a concerned citizen."

I fought the urge to roll my eyes and took a non-flirtatious swig of my drink. If this guy was trying to chat me up, he needed to work on his method.

"Well, concerned citizen, you are correct. I'm nineteen. What are you going to do? Slap some cuffs on me and haul my ass off to Concerned Citizen Jail?"

"I should slap some cuffs on you. But not for drinking underage. For lying to me." The easy and casual smile almost seemed to melt off the other guy's face, morphing into something dark and sensual—and sexy as hell.

"Excuse me?"

"You're not nineteen. You're eighteen. A freshman, if I'm not mistaken."

"How did you now that?"

"I can always tell." He grinned. The dark look was still there, simmering under the surface, and I was admittedly mesmerized. "I'm Dex."

"Chase."

"Chase?" Dex grinned and looked me up and down in that appraising way again. "Let me guess. Freshman, just turned eighteen, and straight out of a small town. You were popular, but not a jock. You weren't a nerd either, even though you like nerd stuff. I'm thinking...the class clown. The one who made everyone laugh, and while you thought you were friends with everyone at the time, you now realize that they weren't only laughing with you, but also at you."

My hand tightened around my cup; I was glad there wasn't much left in it, or I would have sent it sloshing to the floor. He'd just nailed my high school experience and college epiphany in one assessment.

"I'm also thinking good family, very accepting. Middle-class suburbia, if I'm not mistaken."

"How the fuck could you know that?" I managed to sputter. I was usually a freaking gun-slinger when it came to retorts and sassing back, but Dex had reduced me to someone who could barely string a sentence together.

"Because I *was* you," he said simply as he finished off his drink and put the empty cup on the windowsill behind me. His bare arm barely grazed my shoulder as he pulled it back, but the shocks of pure electricity that crackled over my skin were sharp and unexpected. *Fuck.* That was a new reaction to being touched.

"You *were* me?"

"I was. Same story. The funny kid. The one who used humor and jokes to make people like me. It was a shield to keep people away and protect myself. I have the supportive family and the suburban bubble as my childhood home as well. Mom, dad, sister, dog, and even a cat. We're a goddamn Norman Rockwell painting."

"Norman who?" I shook my head to try and clear the cobwebs that were making it impossible for me to process the conversation. "And I have two brothers and no pets."

For some reason, that made Dex smile, and he stepped closer to me. Once again, his arm brushed against mine, and those little crackles of electricity exploded over my skin.

"Ever get tired of it?" he asked casually.

"Tired of what?"

"Of always being the one who makes sure other people are comfortable around you?"

"I don't know what you mean..."

"The jokes. They're a way to make other people comfortable with who you are. You become something non-threatening so everyone else will be comfortable."

"Or they could be a way to make people laugh," I shot back. This conversation was starting to make me uncomfortable—not because Dex was wrong, but because he was scarily right.

"Sure, you keep telling yourself that."

"What's wrong with wanting to make other people comfortable?"

"Nothing. But sometimes being uncomfortable can help you realize who you really are, what you really want."

"Let me guess, you're a psych major?" I quipped lamely. It wasn't much of a joke, but it was all I could muster at the moment. Dex had completely fucked with my equilibrium, and it had been a struggle to even come up with that.

"Mechanical engineering, actually." Dex grinned and stood up straighter, raising himself to his full height. "I'm just really good at reading people."

"So what made you come over and read me?" I had to ask. There were easily a hundred people at this party.

"Your ass in those jeans."

I almost choked on the last sip of my drink. Damn, that was direct.

"And I have a thing for blonds."

"You're taking a bit of a risk, don't you think? Hitting on me in front of all your frat brothers."

"Who says I'm hitting on you?"

I felt the blood rushing to my face as my cheeks flamed hot. He wasn't flirting? How had I misread things?

"Relax, Chase. I'm definitely hitting on you." Dex laughed and lifted his hand so it grazed my cheek in a surprisingly tender way. "You're sexy when you blush."

"Thanks?" I answered stupidly.

I wasn't inexperienced. I'd been going to the one gay club just outside my town for a year before I'd come to college. I'd fucked, been fucked, picked up, and been picked up. I'd never been reduced to a stuttering mess—until now.

"And these aren't my frat brothers. I came with some friends."

"Oh."

What the fuck was wrong with me? Now I could only manage monosyllables?

"Do you want to go somewhere?" Dex asked, licking his full bottom lip as he looked at me.

My eyes followed his tongue, and my half hard dick instantly went to full mast. "Where?"

"My place?"

"'Kay."

Dex grinned and nodded for me to follow him.

Okay. So, I'd come to a party I didn't want to go to for my friend, who'd ghosted me, and now I was leaving with the hottest guy I'd ever talked to after he'd dissected my life in a single conversation.

Tonight had taken a turn I definitely hadn't expected.

I followed Dex out of the crowded frat house, and he slowed when we were on the street so I could fall into step beside him.

"Which residence do you live in?" I asked after the silence had stretched out long enough. It wasn't uncomfortable, per se, but I'd never done well with extended silences in conversation.

"I don't. I live off campus."

"You have roommates?"

"Two sisters. They went home to visit their family this weekend."

"So you're alone?"

"Well, not tonight I'm not." He gave me a dark look as his lips curled into a sexy little smirk. "You're going to be with me."

"True." I shoved my hands in my pockets and bit the inside of my cheek as I thought of what else we could talk about. "How far is it?"

"Only a few minutes. You live in residence?"

"Yes," I said a little too enthusiastically, grateful for the chance to use my big boy words. "I don't mind it. My roommate is never home, and when he is, he's gaming."

"Nice. First year my roommate was a nightmare. He'd drink and get high almost every night. I never saw him do any work, but he'd have these episodes where he'd just freak out from whatever he was on and be up all night talking to himself. More like yelling at himself."

"Shitty. Did you have to deal with him all year?"

"Nah. He left before winter semester. Probably got kicked out. I got a single after that, so it was almost worth it." Dex laughed, and his face practically beamed. It was a stark difference from the dark and sultry looks he'd been giving me all night. "What?" he asked when he caught me looking at him.

"Nothing," I said quickly, dropping my gaze.

"Oh, it's something. What?" he pressed.

"You looked different just then." I shrugged.

"Different?"

"More open? Relaxed, maybe? I don't know."

"Interesting." Dex pursed his lips in a way that made it hard to tell if he was stifling a laugh or calculating something. "We're almost there."

It took me a moment to realize that he meant we were almost at his place, and I glanced around. I'd never been in this neighborhood before. It was nice, but you could tell it was student housing. All of the houses had multiple mailboxes, giving away that they'd been split into apartments, and while there weren't many cars in the driveways, there were plenty of bikes and even a few scooters. The lawns were overgrown, but the properties were clean, and the biggest telltale sign was the assortment of flags and sheets being used as curtains.

"I'm on the top floor." Dex led me up the steps to one of the houses, and I waited as he pulled out his keys to unlock the main door. I followed him up the stairs and waited again while he took care of the door to his apartment.

As soon as we were inside, a flash of anticipation rushed through me. Dex hadn't done more than brush against my arm and touch my cheek, but those simple touches had stirred desire in me, and I wanted to know how it would feel to kiss him.

I wasn't shy when it came to hooking up. I had no trouble making the first move or pushing to see how far things were going to go. If I had been with anyone else, I would have closed the distance between us, pulled him into my arms and kissed him, but something about Dex made me pause.

"You want a drink?" he asked unexpectedly.

"What?"

"A drink. You want one?"

"Um, sure?"

"Beer or water is about all I have. Or coffee creamer if that's your thing," he added with a wink.

"Not my thing." I chuckled. "A beer?"

Dex nodded and disappeared into the kitchen. Before I could follow him, he reappeared with two beers in his hands.

"Thanks." I took the beer he offered and looked around.

It was clean and tidy, and there were little touches like paintings on the walls and candles on the shelves. "Nice place."

"The perk of living with girls. They like to make things pretty."

"I'll have to remember that."

"Come on." He once again nodded for me to follow him down the hall, and we ended up in what I assumed was his bedroom.

It was a pretty basic room. Double bed, dresser, a desk with a laptop and stacks of books, and not much else. I did notice that he had actual curtains up and briefly wondered if that was his touch or his roommates'.

Dex flopped down on his bed in a casual and comfortable way, and I sat next to him, my movements decidedly less casual.

"What're you thinking?" Dex asked after a pause.

"That this is the first time I've gone back to a guy's place and he's offered me a drink before anything else."

"You often go to guys' places and have drinks after you fuck?" He cocked his eyebrow at me in a teasing way, and I felt myself relaxing.

"Well, I certainly don't invite them to my place so..." I shrugged and took a sip of my beer as Dex laughed.

"I like to talk first."

"About what? Politics? Current events?"

"Preferences."

"Preferences?"

"Yeah. Preferences."

"I don't get it."

Dex grinned and took a long swallow of his drink. My eyes were drawn to his Adam's apple, and my mouth watered at the thought of running my tongue over the smooth skin of his neck.

"There are certain things I like that we need to talk about first. They're not something you spring on someone in the moment."

"Now I really don't get it."

"How would you describe yourself? Are you usually the take charge one?"

"You mean when hooking up?"

"Yeah."

"Usually. I like to be in control."

"See, that's my thing too. Only I like to *have* control."

"What do you mean?"

"I like for guys to give me control."

"Like, let you make the first move?"

"Like, let me make all the moves."

I paused, the sweaty beer bottle making my hand cold. "I'm still not getting it."

"Have you ever wondered what it would be like to completely surrender? Where you could just let go and have someone else take over?"

"I guess."

"What about letting them control you and not just the situation?"

"Control me? Like how?"

"Tying you up?"

"Um, I've never tried it before…"

"What about telling you what you can and can't do?"

"Um…I've never really thought about that," I lied.

The truth was I had a pretty good idea of what Dex was talking about, and it was something I'd been wanting to try for a long time. It was true I was usually the more forward one, but that didn't mean I didn't long to be submissive.

The idea of a guy tying me up, telling me what I could and couldn't do, and punishing me for disobeying was way up there on my sexual bucket list and one of my most used fantasies during jerk-off sessions. But I'd never told anyone that, and no one had ever brought it up to me before now.

"Would you..." My voice trailed off as my nerves took over, and the question died before I could get it out.

"Would I what?"

"Punish me?" I had to force the word out, but Dex didn't laugh or look disgusted.

"If you deserved it." He grinned and put his barely touched drink on the floor, and I quickly followed suit.

"I've never done anything like this before," I confessed.

"But you've wanted to."

"Yes."

"Tell me if this is what you want. I won't push too hard right away, and if you need me to stop, tell me. No safe words for your first time."

"Safe words? How often do you do this?"

"You really want to know the answer to that?"

"No," I conceded.

"No, you don't want to do this?"

"No. I mean, no, I don't want to know how often you do this. Yes, I want to do this."

2

———

Dex slid closer to me on the bed. One of his hands closed around the back of my neck as the other gripped my waist, turning me so we were facing each other. The move was sudden, but relatively gentle. And hot as fuck.

He pulled me forward, and I closed my eyes as he leaned in. His lips were warm and soft, and his kiss sent zings of recognition through me. I had no idea how, but it was almost as though my body recognized him, and I instantly relaxed.

My hands gripped his strong waist as his tongue dipped into my mouth and began to tease and massage mine.

Holy shit, he was an amazing kisser. It was as though our surroundings had melted away, and we were the only things left in the world. A low groan rumbled in Dex's throat, and I started to shift so I could straddle him. I needed more.

Using his grip on my neck and waist, Dex maneuvered me mid move, and I found myself flat on my back on his bed. Dex was straddling my hips, pinning my body down as he ravaged my mouth with his kisses.

I might have agreed to let him have control, but that didn't mean I wasn't going to be a full participant. I kissed him with everything I had, wanting to drag the moment out as long as possible.

After what felt like eternity, but still not quite long enough, Dex pulled away and sat back on his heels.

His cheeks were flushed pink, his lips were swollen and red, and his hair was mussed. He looked like he'd been thoroughly kissed, and I imagined I looked about the same. His eyes were bright and focused. It was a weird way to describe them, but that was exactly how they seemed, like his entire focus was on me and the moment.

Dex pulled his shirt off by the collar and tossed it aside before nodding to mine. "Off, now."

I sat up as he got off my legs and pulled my shirt off, tossing it blindly. I started to reach for him, but Dex put his hand on my chest and pushed me back down.

"Oomf." I hadn't been expecting that, but before I could move, Dex was kneeling beside me, one of his hands still on my chest to hold me down as the other worked the button and fly of my jeans open.

I'd been rock hard since before he'd kissed me, and my dick was aching for some sort of stimulation. I tried rocking my hips to force his hand to touch me, but he pulled his hand away and shook his head.

"Stay still," he ordered.

I bit my lip and stopped moving. Part of me wanted to fight back a bit, but a bigger part of me wanted to let Dex do whatever he was planning.

Dex quickly pulled off my shoes and socks before he stripped off my jeans. I was now in nothing but a pair of bright red boxer briefs. My cock was straining against the material, creating a pretty nice tent effect. I hoped Dex would do something to it, but he shook his head.

"Over. On your hands and knees."

My mind spun as he helped me flip over. Wow. We were going right to the fucking? I'd known that agreeing to this would mean I was bottoming, but a little prep would have been nice.

When I was settled on my hands and knees, my ass on full display, Dex undid his belt and slowly pulled it through the loops of his jeans until it was free and swinging in his hand.

"Put your hands together."

I swallowed and did as he said. His voice was low and even, and it made me want to obey him.

Dex wrapped the belt around my wrists, looping and pulling on it until I was firmly tied up. The leather was soft but the edge still bit into my skin. The dichotomy of sensations sent a rush of pleasure through my body, starting at my core and radiating outward.

I'd never been restrained before, and the thought that I was now completely at his mercy made my dick pulse and precum leak into the material of my underwear.

Dex put his hand on my back, gently and slowly tracing down my spine. He stopped at my tailbone, and I bit back a groan as he removed his hand rather than running it over my ass.

My body was screaming for some sort of stimulation. My dick ached, my skin was cold, and my muscles were tight. I needed him to touch me, and before I could stop myself, I blurted out a single word.

"More."

Crack.

I wasn't sure which was more startling—the sound of his

hand smacking against my ass as he spanked me, or the fact that he'd fucking spanked me.

I grunted, some primitive part of me taking over and making me shut the fuck up so he'd do it again.

Slap.

The second spank was just as sudden, but I'd been expecting it, so I was able to take a second to really feel everything that came with the simple but effective move.

The skin of my ass stung, but the nerves underneath were firing on all cylinders, and I could feel that slap radiating everywhere—especially in my dick.

"Fuck."

The third spank was just as hard as the first two, only Dex moved to my other cheek. The same waves of pleasure rocked through me, and more precum leaked into my underwear. I'd never thought that being spanked could feel so good, and I wanted more.

A warm hand ran over the material of my boxer briefs while that same hand was yanking them down so my ass was completely exposed.

"I want you to count them out." Dex's voice was still low and even, but there was a slight rasp to it that told me I wasn't the only one enjoying things.

"One," I grunted as the sharp sound of skin striking skin echoed in the otherwise quiet room. With nothing to absorb any of the impact, the sound was louder, and the pain was sharper.

"Two."

Dex paused his spanking and gently rubbed the palm of his hand over the globes of my ass. The move was tender and soothing, and unexpected.

"Three."

My voice came out in a hoarse whisper. Dex had moved

his hand so he spanked the lower part of my cheek down near where my upper thigh was. It made a duller sound and didn't hurt nearly as much, but I could feel my ass rippling and jiggling from the impact, and there was no missing the low groan Dex let out as he paused to presumably watch.

"Four."

I was in my own world. I wasn't thinking about how I was kneeling ass-up on a guy's bed, letting him spank me and boss me around. I didn't think about how completely out of character this was for me, or how much I'd repressed this fantasy. In this moment I felt no shame, no pressure, and no regrets. I was completely vulnerable, but I'd never felt more free or powerful.

"Five. Six. Seven."

The next three spanks came in such rapid succession they felt like one single hit, and I was barely able to get the words out as my entire body responded.

"Eight. Nine. Ten."

My voice was barely a whisper. The skin of my ass felt like it was on fire, but the rest of my body felt weirdly cold. It was the strangest, most arousing combination I'd ever experienced.

"Please," I begged when Dex didn't move to do anything further.

"Please what?"

His voice was firm and low, but that raspy quality was still there. I desperately wanted to turn to look at him but didn't dare move without being given permission.

"Fuck me."

"No."

My muscles tensed like a plucked guitar string, and I couldn't stop the sounds of protest that escaped my lips as I squeezed my eyes shut. I was wound so fucking tight that I was in physical pain.

"I'm not going to fuck you." Dex ran his hand through my hair and gripped a handful of the strands, his knuckles brushing my scalp. "Yet."

"Fuck!"

Dex had yanked on my hair as he said that last word, sending arousal and hope through me. He wrenched my head so I was facing him, but there was no pain even though the force of the move had almost knocked me off balance.

"Open your eyes," he commanded, and my eyes snapped open.

Dex's eyes were almost glowing in the darkened room. His posture was rigid, and his muscles were tight. Everything about him screamed power and control, and I was mesmerized.

"I'm going to stroke your dick—"

I whimpered in relief but stopped when Dex gave my hair another sharp yet gentle yank.

"But," he let the word hang for a moment before continuing, "you're not going to come until I tell you to. Understand?"

"Yes."

"Good. Now spit."

Dex's free hand appeared in front of my lips, and I spit into his palm. He let go of my hair, and without the extra support, my head fell back down so my chin was almost resting on my chest. I closed my eyes instinctively. It was as though some part of me knew that focusing only on what I was feeling and not distracting myself with sight would make the experience that much more intense and amazing.

His warm hand rested at the back of my neck as the other wrapped around the base of my dick. I was so slick with precum that the added lubrication of my spit made me even more slippery. Dex didn't even have to move his hand to make my shaft slide in his palm. All he had to do was squeeze it.

I let out a primal sounding groan and concentrated on not blowing my load right then and there. I wasn't an edger. I liked to cum fast and hard and only ever held out when I had a partner to think about. I'd never played around with orgasm denial, and I didn't think I'd be able to control myself if that was what Dex had planned.

As Dex slowly ran one hand down my spine, he began stroking my straining cock. The moves were agonizingly slow and deliberate. He stayed close to the base and didn't even graze my sensitive head or the crown.

I wanted to scream in pleasure and frustration. It felt so incredibly amazing, but it wasn't nearly enough.

He stopped moving his hand over my spine when it was resting on the top of my ass. He paused there for a moment before pulling his hand away. He was still barely teasing my dick, and I was dangerously close to cumming.

"Oh, God!" I cried out as Dex pulled his other hand from my cock. I couldn't stop myself from trying to sit up so I could either beg him to finish me or curse him out for being a giant cocktease. At that moment, I could have gone either way.

"Do you have something you want to say to me?"

Dex grabbed another handful of my hair and yanked me down so I was back on my knees. My hands scrambled for purchase on the comforter, and the leather still binding my wrists bit into my skin.

"Well?" he questioned when I didn't say anything. The way he was holding my hair had me at a slightly twisted angle so not only was I at his complete mercy, but he was also the only thing keeping me from face-planting.

"I...I'm sorry."

I knew I could tell him to stop and trusted he would, but the thing was, I didn't want him to stop. I'd reacted instinctively out of frustration, not out of a desire to end things.

"Good boy."

He let go of my hair, and I managed to catch myself before I fell over. Once I was settled, I didn't dare move. I didn't want this to end before he was finished with me.

"Have you ever cum hands free?" Dex asked, his suddenly wet finger tracing the skin around my hole.

"What?"

Between the zings of pleasure rushing through me at his touch and the complete about-face in conversation, I was having a bit of trouble keeping up.

"Have you ever cum hands free?" he repeated patiently.

"Um, no. Never even close."

"You've been fingered before, right?"

"Sure, but that's never happened."

"No one's ever tried?"

"No. That can actually happen outside of porn?"

I heard Dex laugh, a soft and throaty kind of chuckle, and for a second I thought he was laughing at me and my lack of experience when it came to anal foreplay.

"You're about to get your mind blown, Chase."

It was the first time he'd used my name since we'd kissed, and for some reason, it sent a ripple of anticipation through me as I turned to look at him.

Dex spit into his hand, getting most of it near his fingers. He watched me as I watched him, and I was so lost in his gaze I wasn't paying attention to his hand. When he began lightly teasing my hole again, he caught me completely by surprise.

"Fuck." I bit my lip and tried to stifle my cries.

"Be loud. I want to hear you."

"Fuck!"

The tip of Dex's finger penetrated me, and I sucked in a deep breath as I tried to relax my body for what was coming next.

"Oh, God!"

Dex's other hand closed around my still leaking dick as he pushed in slightly, and the dual sensation was almost too much for me.

"That's it. Nice and loud."

He took his time working me open, using plenty of spit and some lube from a small packet he pulled out of his pocket. I was naturally tight, and even though I'd bottomed before, my body still took time to relax.

"Oh my fuck," I moaned as he skillfully worked my cock and pushed two fingers deep inside me. "Ah!"

He'd found my prostate and was hitting it at the perfect angle with every thrust as he finger fucked me.

"No, don't stop!" I cried out in desperation when he stopped stroking my dick and let go of me. I was so close I could barely think straight. My legs were shaking, my abdomen was cramping, and I *needed* to cum.

"Relax and take it." Dex's voice was low but loud, and it penetrated my pleasure-filled haze. "Feel it, let go, and just go with it."

What he was asking sounded impossible in the state I was in, but I somehow managed to find enough control to do it. Doing so, I unfortunately used up all of whatever control I had left, and from that moment on I was beyond coherence.

Words and cries tumbled from my lips, and I had no idea, nor did I care, what I was saying. My hips rocked, my legs shook, and my muscles tightened to a point where I was sure they'd snap.

I was in a place that consisted only of pleasure and need. Up was down, left was right, and pain was pleasure. I had no idea how long I was in this place—it could have been seconds or minutes—but suddenly something inside me snapped, and the built-up pleasure in my body finally exploded in a reality-numbing crescendo.

Fireworks went off behind my eyes as the blood rushed to my ears. I'd never felt anything like it before, and it wasn't until I felt Dex's warm hand on my back, gently rubbing in circles, that I started to come down from my orgasm.

"What. The. Fuck. Happened?" I asked, gasping breaths punctuating each word.

"Lay down." Dex nudged me until I flopped over in an ungraceful heap. "Just take a second, Chase. Process."

"'Kay."

Dex quickly pulled the belt off my hands and stripped off his jeans and briefs.

His dick was perfect. Long and thick with a slight curve to the left. The head was flushed purple, and precum dripped from his tip. He was hard as a steel pipe, and as he began stroking himself, something inside me seemed to snap, and I was fully aware of my body and in control again.

"Cum on me." I rolled onto my back and wiggled closer to him.

"Yeah?" He grinned and shifted closer to the bed. "You want my cum?"

"Please." I nodded eagerly and put my hands above my head and held them together. I might not have been tied up anymore, but I still wanted that illusion as he jerked off on me.

"Such a good little cumslut. Next time this will be your greedy little hole."

I groaned and opened my mouth. If he wasn't going to creampie me tonight, I sure as hell wanted him to give me a facial.

"That's fucking hot." Dex was staring at me as he furiously worked his cock, and it was at that moment that I realized I was still hard. That was new. I usually went soft right away after an orgasm, especially a big one.

"Please, cum on me."

"Beg for it. Beg for my cum."

"Please. Please, I need you to cum on me. I need to feel it." I was almost whimpering as I begged, and I figured it was an after-effect of the domination and orgasm he'd given me because this was completely out of character for me. I didn't mind a facial, but I'd never begged for one.

I opened my mouth wider and pressed my wrists together to mimic the feeling of being restrained. Dex let out a low groan, his eyes sweeping over my body as he leaned over me.

"Fuck!" he cried out, and I instinctively closed my eyes as he emptied his warm load all over my face. Some of it got in my mouth, and I greedily swallowed it before running my tongue over my lips to lap up every drop that I could.

"Fucking hell, you're so hot." Dex was still gripping his softening cock with one hand as he watched me, and it was then that I realized my own dick was finally going soft as well.

After a moment, Dex broke our eye contact and turned away, and that was the moment all my self-conscious thoughts came rushing back to me.

What the fuck had I become just now? Begging him to cum on my face, letting him not only control my body, but also my pleasure like that? I'd just met the guy, and I'd spent our first hook up on my hands and knees and nearly out of my mind with pleasure and delirium.

"Here, wipe down with this." Dex handed me a t-shirt and climbed into bed next to me. I was grateful for the contact but embarrassed as hell.

I wiped my face and the top of my chest and tossed the shirt aside.

"I should go."

"Not yet." Dex stopped me with a hand on my chest and gently pushed me back on the bed. "You need to process that."

"Why?" I tried to brush him off. "It was fun, it's over. What's to process?"

"Chase, you went into subspace."

"Into what?"

"Subspace. It's a state of mind a submissive partner gets into when a session is really intense. It's like you go to another place and completely give into what's happening."

"Is that not normal?"

"It is, and it usually means you enjoyed it. But there can be a bit of a crash after you come out of it. That's very normal."

My skin suddenly went cold, and I started shaking slightly.

"Just take a minute and process it. Ask me anything you need to." Dex wrapped his arm around me and pulled me close. The heat from his body was welcome, and I started to feel more in control almost immediately.

"So that was normal? I didn't get all weird?"

"Everyone reacts differently. As long as you enjoyed it, then it was normal."

"Where did you learn about this stuff?" I couldn't help asking. Dex was only three years older than me, but that had been eons beyond my experience.

"I told you, I used to be you." He chuckled. "I met someone when I was a freshman who saw beneath the persona I projected and showed me what I really wanted."

"And that's how you saw it in me?"

"Pretty much."

I wasn't sure of the terms, but I was curious if he still liked to be the submissive one. "Do you...do both?"

"Switch? No. Not anymore. I did when I was learning, but it's not what I want anymore."

"Oh."

"Why? Would you want to switch?"

"Um." I paused and thought about it. Every fantasy I'd ever had revolved around me giving up my power and being the one who was controlled, and now that I'd experienced it, I was sure that was the role I wanted to keep having. It was hard to even imagine switching so that I was the one with the control. "No. I don't think so."

"Feeling better?"

"Yes. Embarrassed, but better," I admitted.

"Why?"

"Because you have to take care of me like this. I feel weak."

"Chase, I already told you, this is the crash from subspace. It's normal. Besides, aftercare is a huge part of dom/sub play."

I didn't quite believe him but let it go. No point making a bigger deal out of it than I already was.

"Would you want to do this again?" he asked after a pause.

"Like exactly this or hook up?"

"Either or."

"Yes."

"Yes?" Dex chuckled and gave me a little squeeze that sent a rush of calming heat through me. "To which one?"

"Both?"

"Both." He nodded and pressed a kiss against my neck. The move was completely unexpected, and it made me feel safe enough that the last of my insecurities seemed to melt away.

"Do you want to stay here tonight?" Dex asked, his voice getting thick with sleep.

"Yeah, thanks."

"Good." Dex kicked up the sheets and pulled them over us as we shifted and wiggled until we were up on the pillows.

I half expected him to roll away from me and settle in his own space, but he stayed against my back and held me. I wasn't used to being the little spoon, but I had to admit, I liked it.

3

———

Things the next morning weren't awkward or weird, but it wasn't something out of a movie either. I woke up as Dex was getting out of bed, and we had a simple, "Hey, how are you doing today?" kind of conversation as we got dressed.

The only part of the morning that was strange was when Dex took my number but didn't make a move to give me his. After a slightly awkward standoff, I asked if he was going to give it to me, and he said something that sent shivers of anticipation up my spine:

"I'll give it to you when you earn it."

We kissed briefly at the door to his apartment, and he watched me walk down the stairs.

That was it. It seemed a bit weird after what had happened last night, but I was grateful my self-doubt hadn't kicked back in, and I was feeling good about everything. Dex may have been able to strip me bare, both emotionally and physically, but today I felt like myself again.

It didn't take long to get to my dorm, and it was still early enough that there weren't many people up and about. I took a long shower, marveling at the nearly perfect red handprints that were bruised into my ass. They didn't hurt, and every time I looked at them I remembered just how good it had felt to get them.

After wasting a little too much water with my Hollywood shower, I turned off the taps and quickly dried off. I could hear someone grunting in a shower stall nearby and rolled my eyes. Some guys just couldn't help jerking off in the shower even if other dudes were in the area.

After I was dry and had gathered all my things, I wrapped my towel around my waist and headed into the hallway. I had just gotten back to my room when my phone vibrated against the wood of the desk I'd tossed it on before I'd gone for my shower.

I rushed over to pick it up, hoping I'd see an unknown number on the screen and it would be a text from Dex, but my friend Paige's picture was staring at me.

I'm mad at you.

I rolled my eyes as I read her text and sat down on the corner of my bed. Paige was as dramatic as she was silly, so I knew this was either a build up for some kind of joke or something less than serious.

What did I do this time?

Paige sent back a picture of a puppy with angry eyes and the words "you know what you did" over its head, and I couldn't help laughing.

Then I'm sorry...for whatever it is that I know I did.

You suck.

We both know I do.

Jerk! I'm trying to be mad at you. Don't make me laugh.

I can't help being hilarious.

Stop being so damn adorable.

Can't do that either.

Well I'm mad for a real reason and you're making me want to forgive you.

What did I do?

If Paige was saying there was a real reason, then I'd fucked up.

I came by for our breakfast date and you weren't there.

Oh shit. Paige and I had set up this breakfast date earlier in the week since it was the only time this weekend we were both free at the same time.

This time it was my turn to send a gif, and I picked one of a guy falling on his knees in front of a pissed-off looking woman with "forgive me" flashing over the picture.

No.

Pretty please? I'm both adorable and hilarious.

Maybe. You better have had a good reason.

I have a reason, not sure if you'd consider it good.

Did you hook up?

I paused. Part of me wanted to tell Paige all about last night in graphic detail, but the other part me wanted to keep the night to myself. I trusted Paige and usually told her everything, but this felt too personal. This wasn't just telling her I messed around with someone. This would be telling her that I was into BDSM, and I wasn't ready for that step yet.

I met someone and crashed at his place.

That was as neutral as I could make it without lying to her, and the text set off a flurry of gifs, pictures, and emojis. Paige was always enthusiastic about my dating life since she was in a long-distance relationship with her high school boyfriend. She said that her forced celibacy made her need to live vicariously through me.

When the messages calmed, I sent her back the hug and kiss emojis and promised to make it up to her and give her all the details later. She had to work in less than an hour, and I had some major cramming to do for the history test I had on Monday that I'd been ignoring for the last week.

Four hours later, my stomach was rumbling, and my brain was fried. I'd been studying like crazy for my test, but I was at the point where everything was blurring together, and I needed to take a break.

I didn't really want to eat in the dining hall—the weekend food kind of sucked compared to what they served during the week—but I was broke and lazy and didn't feel like going off-campus or to one of the restaurants on the other side of campus. I thought about texting Trey to see what the hell was up since I still hadn't heard from him, but I decided against it. He'd ghosted me. It was his turn to reach out.

I randomly bumped into a group of people I knew as I was heading to the dining hall, and we struck up a casual conversation as we made our way to the building. I didn't mind eating alone, but it was nice to have other people to talk to since I knew I wouldn't be seeing much of my roommate this weekend and could use the human interaction.

The selection was dismal, and I ended up getting a chicken burger with fries. Not the healthiest choice, but it was better than the lumpy mac and cheese and waxy pizza that was also available. We'd shown up at an off time, and pretty much everything else was empty and in the process of being refilled. I didn't feel like waiting for better options, so I got my food and went to sit down.

The rest of the group I'd walked over with joined me,

and between eating and checking our phones, there wasn't much conversation.

I was almost done eating when my phone vibrated, interrupting the game I'd been playing. I had a text from an unknown number.

I exited out of my game and opened the text, my heart beating the slightest bit faster as I did. Was it Dex?

What are you doing?

I paused. There was no indication of whom the message was from. I didn't make a habit of giving out my number all willy nilly, but that didn't mean it wasn't a wrong number.

Eating lunch. Who's this?

Who do you think it is?

Dex?

Ding ding ding.

I assumed that meant I'd gotten it right and paused.

What are you doing? I asked when he stayed silent.

Nothing important.

I thought you said I'd have to work to get your number? This wasn't exactly hard.

This isn't my number, it's an anonymous one. I can dump it at any time. There really is an app for everything.

Well, shit. That was a twist I hadn't considered.

You'll have to work to get my real number.

So what do I need to do?

You like being controlled in person, do you like being controlled from afar?

I don't know what you mean.

Text this number when you get back to your room and I'll show you.

I didn't respond because something told me he wasn't expecting, or wanting, an answer.

This was new. I'd always had fantasies about being

spanked and restrained and controlled during sex, but the idea of someone controlling me through a phone was new. I wasn't opposed to it, per se, but I needed more information.

If he was going to tell me to crawl around my room like a dog and drink from a bowl on the floor, he could go fuck himself. I'd seen that a few times while searching domination porn, and I didn't care how good the orgasm had been last night, I wasn't into that kind of thing.

A part of me was still feeling defiant, and instead of rushing back to my room, I took my time finishing my lunch and even took the time to have a cup of coffee. When I really couldn't stall anymore, I headed back to my building.

I needed to hit the gym tomorrow. It was always busy as fuck on Saturdays, but the crowds were doable on Sundays. As long as I wasn't hungover, I'd make sure I went. I made a to-do list in my head as I headed over to my building and took the stairs up to my room. It wasn't a full workout, but running up sixteen flights of stairs was a good way to get the blood pumping and work out my legs and ass.

When I got to my room, I wrote down my list and flopped on my bed. Unless I started studying or made an unnecessary trip to the bathroom, I was out of ways to stall.

Hey. It wasn't the cleverest text, but it was as much effort as I was putting into this until I knew more.

Took a while.

I was hungry.

Is your roommate home?

No.

Good.

What exactly are we going to do here?

Have you ever heard of JOI?

No. What's that?

Jerk off instructions.

Okay...

I'm going to tell you what to do, and you're going to do it.

I had no idea how he was planning to do this, but the idea that he'd be in control of my pleasure while I was jerking off was actually kind of hot.

Okay.

Okay like okay let's do it?

Yeah.

That's what I like to hear.

So, are you going to call me or something?

No. I'm just going to write what you should do and you're going to obey.

What if I don't? You'd never know.

True, but you would. You can cheat if you want but you won't get as much out of it. I can only control you if you let me.

Sounds like I have the control here.

You'd think, but no.

Are you sure?

Do you want to cum or argue semantics?

Cum.

My phone stayed quiet, and for a second I thought that meant I'd answered wrong or Dex had changed his mind. Then I saw the little bubbles that indicated he was typing. After what seemed like forever, a message appeared on my screen.

Get on your knees and put the phone down on the bed in front of you. Don't touch your phone until you cum.

I moved into position and waited as the bubbles appeared again. This was kind of a random position to choose, but whatever. He was the boss.

Rub your hand over your pants, squeezing your cock as you do. Move slow and pay attention to your dick getting harder. Really feel it.

I'd changed into sweatpants after my shower, so it didn't take long for my cock to start thickening. I did as he said and concentrated on my dick as I got hard. It was different. I usually didn't notice the stages of getting an erection because I was so focused on actually having one, but this time I noticed everything. The way I got hard from the base up. How the entire area heated up and made my hand warm. Even the rubbing of the material of my pants against my briefs and how that sensation turned into a completely new one as I rubbed the fabric against my dick.

"Fuck." I let out a breath and looked down at my phone for his next instruction.

When you're completely hard I want you to get naked except for one layer of clothes on the bottom.

I assumed he didn't mean leaving on my socks, so I stripped off my shirt and sweatpants until I was left in only my briefs. It felt a little weird to be so exposed, but I was in my room, so it wasn't like I had anything to worry about.

Now grip your cock over your clothes and stroke yourself through them. Do it slow. Tease yourself, don't try to make yourself cum.

I actually really enjoyed over-the-clothes touching, and it was one of the things that got me hot fast. Dex would have no way of knowing that, so he wouldn't realize that this was exactly how I'd try to make myself cum if I was alone.

That's it. Keep stroking.

"Fuck, yes," I moaned loudly and then bit my lip to silence myself. I might have been alone, but the walls of this place were paper thin, and I didn't need the rest of my floor to know I was jerking off.

Now pull your cock free. Don't touch it. I want you to look at it and imagine my mouth is around you. Imagine I'm sucking you exactly the way you like it. Imagine me working as hard as I can to make you cum down my throat.

"Jesus fuck." I couldn't stop the groan that escaped my lips at his words. Just reading it was enough to make precum drip from my tip; actually imagining it would be torture if I couldn't touch myself.

I linked my hands and put them behind my head as I looked down at my dripping cock. I couldn't visually picture Dex sucking me off, but I could imagine the sensations it would cause, and I had to force myself to stay exactly as I was and not reach down to start jerking.

I'd never realized that not touching myself could be just as pleasurable as actually stroking, and I had to double up my efforts to not groan or move.

Now imagine I'm fingering you. I'm tracing my finger over your hole. It's slick and wet and you're so ready for it. I don't even have to push hard and suddenly I'm inside you as I suck your cock.

"Holy shit."

I could almost feel his fingers since the memory of him fingering me last night was still fresh in my mind. At this point, my body was tight as a drum. I unconsciously widened my stance, almost as though I was trying to open up for him, like he was actually in the room with me.

I'm rubbing your spot as I bring your dick all the way down my throat. I'm hitting it over and over again as I swallow every inch of you. You want to cum so bad your body is screaming for it, but you know it's not time so you fight it.

I was physically shaking from the effort of not grabbing my dick so I could cum all over my bedspread. I'd never known words could have such an effect on me, and as much as I wanted to cum, he was right. It wasn't time, so I had to fight it.

Now I have you bent over. You're on your hands and knees and I'm behind you. You're begging me to fuck you. You feel my cock against your tight little hole, and then I start pushing in.

I fell forward so I was bent over, my dick as hard as steel as I held myself up. I was moaning and groaning and couldn't have stopped if I wanted to. My dick was leaking precum all over my bed, and the pleasure rolling around inside me was so strong it hurt. I didn't want it to end. Not yet.

I'm inside you. My dick is deep in your ass and I'm fucking you. I'm going hard and fast, my legs slapping against your perfect ass as I hold your hips so I can pull you back and fuck you even harder. You've never gotten it this hard before and you're screaming for me.

"Fuck, fuck, fuck, fuck, fuck." I shook my head and balled my hands into tight fists. I would have given anything for that to have been happening in real life and not just as words on a screen.

Grab your dick and fuck your hand. Use your hips like you want me to use mine. Fuck your hand as hard and as fast as you want. Every stroke is what I'm doing to you.

At this point I would have had to bury my face in a pillow to keep myself quiet, but I was beyond giving a fuck if people knew I was getting off. It wasn't like I didn't have to hear them at all hours of the night and day.

I spit in my hand and did what Dex said. I pistoned my hips as hard and as fast as I could, making sure to keep my hand still. The feeling was incredible. I could almost feel ghostlike sensations of Dex's dick inside me, fucking me in time as I fucked my hand.

It was like nothing I'd ever experienced, and I felt myself hurdling toward my release in record time.

STOP.

Let go of your dick and stay completely still. DO NOT CUM.

It took every ounce of control I had left, but I did as Dex commanded.

My balls were so high and tight it felt as though they'd disappeared into my body. My muscles were contracting, and my mind was getting close to that delirious point again. Getting edged was one thing—being told to edge myself was a whole new level of intense.

When Dex didn't text again, I started to war with myself. He wasn't here to see what I was doing, and he wasn't texting. He'd never know if I gave in and came, but it had been so good up to this point I could have been robbing myself if I didn't keep listening to him.

I wanted to cum so badly, but I wanted to see this through more. I wanted to be good for Dex.

Thankfully, all that thinking and inner turmoil brought my arousal down to a level that was manageable, and I was able to start relaxing. My dick was screaming for my touch, but I could hold off.

Now start all over again. I want you to grip your dick and fuck your hand. Imagine I'm fucking you and that's my hand around your cock as I force you to move. Every time I fuck you, you'd fuck my hand.

Goddamn, that was hot. I'd never been fucked that hard before, but I wanted to be.

Don't cum until I tell you. Keep edging yourself. Stop when you have to, but only until you can handle it again. My next text will be your command to cum. Do not stop until you get my text.

For the next eleven minutes I was forced to edge myself. The only reason I knew it was eleven minutes was because I kept an eye on the time counter on my phone. I was having trouble concentrating on anything other than that damn time count as I slipped deeper and deeper into the realm of pure pleasure. It was torture, pure, blissful torture, to keep bringing myself up to that moment before orgasm and then to let go of my dick and force myself to stay there and not cum. Over and over again I found myself hovering at that moment, and it got harder and harder to stop myself from going over.

Cum for me.

My hips bucked as my hand furiously stroked my cock. I cried out in the silent room, and within seconds all the pent-up pleasure in my body exploded in a mind-numbing, body-shattering orgasm.

My hot load spilled over my hand and onto my bedspread as my head began to spin, and I was pulled into that place where only feelings exist. I felt every spasm, every twitch, and every aftershock that rippled through my body from the base of my feet to the roots of my hair.

When the sensations finally started to dissipate, I was able to open my eyes, and my surroundings slowly came into focus.

"Holy fuck," I whispered as I blinked, trying to get enough focus so I could look at my phone.

Did you do as I said?

I picked up my phone with shaking hands and typed a simple "yes." It was about as much as I could manage at the moment.

Did you cum hard?

I sent back another "yes" as a few more of my faculties came back to me.

Send a picture of your load to this number.

I was about to flip to my camera when a phone number appeared in the next text. Was that his real number?

I took a picture of my messy bedspread and hand and quickly sent it to the number he'd given me. I had a brief worry that he was making me send a lewd picture to a random phone and I was about to shock some unsuspecting person, but I pushed past it. Dex was a dom, he wasn't an asshole.

Wanting use of both of my hands, I wiped my cum-covered hand on my bedspread and shifted so I could sit on a dry section of my bed. Making the wet spot was always fun, but sitting in it afterward was not.

My phone lit up, and the number I'd sent the picture to flashed on my screen. Dex was calling me.

"How did you like that?" he asked after I'd answered.

"That was fucking hot."

"You liked it?" he chuckled, and I couldn't help grinning.

"Oh, yeah." I paused—there was one thing I couldn't help wondering about. "Did you cum too?"

"Yeah. That's what I was doing while I made you wait. You weren't going to cum until I did."

"Hot. As. Fuck."

"It was."

"So this is your real number?"

"It is. I'd say you earned it."

"I'd hope so."

"Think you could cum again today?"

"You mean now?"

"Not now, later." Dex laughed.

"Yeah. Twice in a day isn't anything new for me."

"Good. Come over tonight?"

"Sure. Yeah, sounds good," I said, trying and failing to not sound too eager.

"Great. Around nine work for you?"

"That's good." I nodded, aware that he couldn't see me over the phone. I was supposed to meet up with some friends to play a strategy game tonight but was definitely going to be cancelling to see Dex again. There was no way a board game was going to beat out another orgasm like the last two.

"Great, see you then."

"Are you..." I trailed off, not sure how or if I should finish my thought.

"Am I what?" he prompted.

"Are you gong to fuck me tonight?"

"Do you want me to fuck you tonight?"

"Yes!"

"Then we'll see. I might, but I might not. Depends on what mood I'm in."

I bit my lip to stop myself from replying. I had no idea if this was part of his mental games or if he truly meant he hadn't decided yet, but I figured it was best to just let it go.

"So, see you at nine?" I said, hoping I sounded both breezy and neutral.

"See you then."

Dex ended the call, and I was left holding my phone. I was still sitting on my bed, naked except for my briefs, which were resting under my ass with my dick and balls sticking out over the front.

Dex had managed to blow my mind in person and over the phone, and he still hadn't fucked me. As much as I was looking forward to that actually happening, I couldn't help wondering if I'd survive it.

4

Studying after that phone call was next to impossible, and I was glad I'd done a small amount of studying before. I didn't know what to do with myself.

After puttering around my room trying to find something that could hold my attention for more than two minutes, I gave up and put my gym clothes on. The lines and crowds at the student gym would be insane right now, but it was better than driving myself crazy in my room.

Even with the mass of students who also had the brilliant idea to be there during the gym's busiest time, I was able to get a good workout in. I got a decent leg workout by taking the stairs every time I went up to my room, so I worked on my core and some cardio. In hindsight, it probably wasn't the best idea considering having sore stomach muscles wasn't the sexiest feeling, but the need to distract my mind and body won out, and I pushed myself.

I was sore and satisfied when I headed back to my room and took the stairs as fast as I could for one last little push. After taking my second shower of the day and doing some extra prep, I checked my phone and saw that Trey had texted.

I brushed past his apology for ghosting me and told him I was going to be bailing on our game night. He didn't ask why, and I didn't tell him, but it was obviously for a hook up, and there was no doubt in my mind that he knew this. Trey asked me to meet him at a sandwich shop for dinner, so after grabbing my keys and slipping on my shoes, I headed out the door.

"What's up with you tonight?" Trey asked as we sat at one of the bench-like tables in the back corner of the shop.

"What do you mean?" I unwrapped my sandwich and lifted it so I could take a big bite. I was suddenly starving.

"You just seem like you're waiting for something. You have a date tonight?"

"Not a date, exactly," I said once I'd swallowed my too-big bite.

"Then what?"

"Just meeting a guy."

"But not a date?"

"I usually like a man to take me out somewhere for a date. Or have something planned other than fucking."

"Valid points." Trey laughed and picked up his drink. "So, who's the guy?"

"I met him at the party last night."

"Really? Nice. You like him?"

"He's...interesting." I didn't have a better word to use to describe Dex. And while I liked how he made me feel, it was way too early to know if I liked him beyond fooling around and discovering a new facet of my sexuality.

"Interesting? Okay." Trey nodded, signaling that he knew the conversation was over. "Was Nevaeh at the party last night?"

"I didn't see her. Where'd you end up?"

"Got sidetracked."

"Translation, you were gaming and completely lost track of time."

Trey rolled his eyes and then grinned. "Think you'd have met that guy if I'd been there pining after a girl who'll never notice me? You should be thanking me. You're getting laid because of me. You should think of that later, when you're with him."

"Gross." I tossed a balled up napkin at him and laughed. "Instant boner killer."

Trey tossed the napkin back and laughed along with me. He wasn't wrong about how I might not have met Dex last night if he'd been there, but there was no way in hell I was going to admit that. And I sure as hell wasn't going to be thinking about that later on when I was at Dex's place.

I STOOD on the street looking up at Dex's building. I wasn't nervous. In the hours leading up to our meeting and the entire walk over, I'd been a bundle of nerves. But now that I was here and about to see him again, the nerves had dissipated and been replaced with flutters of anticipation.

Even though I was about to go inside and submit to a man I'd only just met, I felt empowered. I was exploring a part of me that I'd hidden for as long as I'd known it was there. I'd been ashamed and embarrassed about the things that turned me on, but now I realized that there were other people like me out there, and there was nothing wrong with liking something most people would consider outside of the norm.

My phone vibrated in my pocket, and I pulled it out, half

expecting a message from Paige asking me for details about last night.

It wasn't Paige. It was Dex.

You an architecture student?

No. That had been a random question.

Civil engineering?

No, political science. Why?

Because you're staring at my house like it's either a work of art or you're afraid it's going to swallow you whole.

I swung my gaze toward the front door and saw Dex standing there, silhouetted by the dark hallway.

I shoved my phone back in my pocket and headed up to meet him.

"You know, a part of me thought you were going to text back after you saw me." Dex led the way up to his apartment, and I trailed behind him, not bothering to pretend like I wasn't staring at his ass.

I hoped he was at least a little bit verse because just the thought of fucking him was enough to make my ears hot and my face flush. With him, it wouldn't be anything kinky, I just wanted to have vanilla sex where I got to be the top. Flipping would be fun, too.

"You with me, Chase?"

"What?" I snapped my eyes up to find Dex staring at me as we headed into his apartment.

"You were in your own little world there." He grinned, nodding to the kitchen. "Drink?"

"No, thanks."

"I'm not exactly thirsty for a drink either." Dex headed toward his bedroom, and I fell into step behind him. "So, what were you thinking about just now?"

"Nothing."

"Anytime someone says nothing, they really mean it's

something." Dex sat down and patted the comforter for me to sit with him.

"I was just thinking about us having sex."

"What kind of sex?"

"Like, normal? I mean, vanilla sex."

"And what did this look like?" Dex leaned back on his hands and cocked his head at me.

"Um, just fucking. No kink or anything."

"Who's topping?" Dex pressed.

"We both do?"

"Are you asking me or telling me?" Dex chuckled.

"Telling you?"

"So, flip fucking? I can get behind that. Or in front of it."

My dick instantly went from half interested to standing at full mast, and I had to shift and rearrange myself to make sure I didn't end up with a zipper print on my shaft.

"Really?"

"Sure. I don't like being a sub anymore, but I'm always down to flip fuck."

"So we could do both? Kinky and vanilla?"

"If you want to." Dex sat up straight, a serious look coming over his face. "What do you think is going on here?"

"Honestly? We're two guys hooking up and doing some kinky shit."

"Is that what you want?"

I felt very on-the-spot but decided to just blurt out the first thing that came to mind. If I couldn't be honest with Dex about what I wanted, then I really shouldn't have been submitting to him the way I was.

"It's part of what I want."

"What's the other part?"

"I'd like to get to know you while we experiment with

stuff. I don't know if that fucks up the whole dom thing, but—"

"I like to play with being a dom. I don't live the lifestyle." Dex shook his head. "I'm only like that when it comes to sex."

"I was wondering about that."

"I have to be honest with you. I'm not looking for anything serious right now."

"Who said anything about serious?" I playfully elbowed Dex in the side and laughed when he let out a squeak of surprise. "I was thinking more like friends."

It was true I wanted to get to know him, but I wasn't looking for serious either. A fuck friend was really the best of both worlds, so that was what I wanted.

"I can do friends."

"So, we're cool?"

"Yeah." Dex grinned and reached under his bed to pull out a large shoebox. "What do you think of the toys I picked out for tonight?"

I peered into the box, and my mouth dropped open. There was a pair of handcuffs, what looked like a leather gag, a lighter, a thin-tapered candle, lube, and a condom.

"I can guess what most of that is for, but the candle?"

"Ever spill wax on your hand?"

"Sure. Wait. You want to use wax on me?"

"I do."

Wax wasn't something I'd ever thought of experimenting with before, but the thought did intrigue me. I'd spilled wax on my hands like Dex had said, and even though it had hurt as it was happening, the sensations had dulled as the wax had dried. It hadn't hurt my hands, and I had to wonder how it would feel on other parts of my body.

"Where would you be putting it?" I asked, after a

disturbing imagine of my dick being covered in wax flashed in my mind.

"Just your chest and maybe a little on your stomach. Not your junk."

"I guess the look of panic that must have been on my face gave that thought away."

"A little." Dex pulled the candle out and spun it around in his hand like people do with drumsticks. "You can say no if you're not into it."

"Why not." I shrugged. "I've already had you spank my ass raw, I might as well have you pour wax on me."

"I left marks?" Dex perked up.

"Yeah. I saw them in the shower. They're almost hand-print-shaped, too, so there's no pretending they're something else."

"Show me."

Dex's voice deepened, and the look in his eyes went from excited to primal. Both of those reactions sent a spike of pleasure up my spine.

I stood and turned around so my back was to him before opening my pants so I could slip them down. I held my pants so they hung around my upper thighs with one hand and reached back to pull my briefs down with the other.

I felt a pair of warm hands on my waist and paused. A moment later those hands were gripping the top of my briefs and slipping them down over the globes of my ass.

"Oh, yes," Dex breathed out appreciatively. "That's fucking hot."

"Yeah. It is," I agreed.

"Turn around."

I spun around and saw that Dex had the handcuffs in one of his hands as he looked me up and down.

"Strip."

He didn't need to tell me twice. I eagerly pulled off my clothes and tossed them aside. When I was completely naked, I put my wrists out so Dex could cuff them.

The smile of approval he gave me sent a flush over my skin. I'd never been cuffed before, but the moment he snapped them closed over my wrists, I decided that I was a fan.

There was something about the way they clicked as he closed them, the cold metal against my skin and the weight of them, that reminded me that they were on but I couldn't get free no matter how hard I tried. It was incredibly erotic. The belt had been hot, but this brought things to a whole new level.

Dex motioned for me to kneel in front of him, and I dropped to my knees. I assumed he was going to pull his dick out so I could suck it, but instead he held up the gag. I opened my mouth so he could slip the leather bit between my lips and waited as he secured it behind my head.

With my hands bound and my mouth gagged, I felt completely at Dex's mercy. And I loved it.

"Do you know how to snap your fingers?"

It took me a second to follow the abrupt change in conversation, and I blinked before nodding. Didn't everyone know how to snap their fingers?

"You can't talk, so if it's too much and you need me to stop, snap your fingers a few times. Okay?"

I nodded. I wasn't planning on tapping out, but it was nice to have an escape plan just in case things got too intense.

"Good. Now lie down and put your hands up above your head," he commanded.

It was a bit of a struggle, but I lay on my back with my hands up like he'd told me. My dick had softened a bit while he'd told me about our safe signal, but at his command it was quickly back to being rock hard and dripping precum.

Dex reached up and tied a rope that was fastened to the headboard around the chain of the cuffs, effectively anchoring me in place.

Now, I was completely helpless and vulnerable, and I watched as Dex stripped down to a pair of sexy black boxer briefs. A shiver of anxiety settled over me as I watched him pick up the candle and light it. I wasn't afraid, but I was for sure apprehensive.

He held the candle over my chest and tilted it to the side. We both watched in rapt fascination as the first drop of wax fell from the candle and landed on my pec, right next to my nipple.

"Ugh." I jerked slightly at the contact and let out a grunt of surprise. It didn't hurt. There was a sting as the wax landed, but within seconds it cooled until it was warm and solid.

Dex alternated between looking at my body where the wax was falling to looking at my face to see my reactions. I didn't hold back or try to censor myself. I let out every moan and grunt that felt natural and embraced the sensations.

"It looks like you're covered in cum." Dex blew out the candle and tossed it aside as he stared down at me. "Like you begged for me to cum all over you again."

I nodded to tell him I liked that idea, and he ran one finger down my chest, displacing some of the wax as he did.

"Flip over on your hands and knees. I want that perfect ass in the air and ready for me," Dex said as he moved off me. I didn't hesitate and immediately flipped over and steadied myself on all fours as I arched my back to make my ass even more prominent.

This position made the metal of the handcuffs bite into

my skin, but that only added to my arousal. I had no idea what Dex was going to do to me, and I was so wound up there were very few things I wouldn't have let him do.

Warm hands pressed against the globes of my ass, spreading me open. I sucked in a breath and closed my eyes, wanting to fully immerse myself in the sensations of whatever was coming.

I wasn't sure what I'd expected, but a warm tongue hadn't been at the top of my list. Rimming wasn't something I had a lot of experience in. I'd done it and had it done to me, but this felt different. Dex wasn't just diving in and trying to work me open, he was teasing me with small strokes of his tongue.

The gag made it impossible to form words, so all of the sounds falling from my lips were variations of the same grunt of pleasure. Dex was going just slowly and gently enough that it wasn't enough. The sensitive skin surrounding my hole tingled, and zings of pleasure shot through me, but I needed more.

"Argh!"

I let out a choked scream as Dex's tongue speared into me, pressing right past my outer ring of muscles. It felt so fucking good, and I continued to cry out as he did it over and over again, mimicking fucking me.

Crack.

I hadn't been expecting that spank, and the sharp pain mixed together with the pleasure Dex's tongue was creating had a whole new sensation washing over me. It was the perfect blend of pain and pleasure, and my dick began leaking in earnest as I not only enjoyed it, but reveled in it.

Crack. Crack. Crack.

The rapid succession of the next three spanks was almost too much for me to handle, and I wiggled my ass slightly, trying to tell him I was close without stopping him. He'd already proven he could make me cum from fingering; I wouldn't put it past him to be able to do it from rimming too.

Dex seemed to understand my hint and pulled back. I was both relieved and devastated because it was too much while not being enough. Jesus, would any of this ever *really* be enough?

I heard the snick of a cap opening, and a moment later slick fingers were tracing over my hole.

"I was going to finger you right up to the moment of orgasm again and edge the fuck out of you, but I can't wait to bury my cock in your ass," Dex said, his voice raspy and strained.

I whimpered in agreement. That was exactly where I wanted his cock to be.

One lubed-up finger pushed into me, then a second. I was so turned on it was easy to relax, but I still felt it as he stretched me.

I was slipping into that place again, the one where pain and pleasure felt equally amazing, and time and space didn't exist. My head was hanging low, and my hands were balled into fists as I gripped the comforter.

I was ready. So fucking ready for him.

Dex removed his fingers from me, and I cried out at the loss, but they were immediately replaced by the broad head of his cock.

He pressed into me, moving slowly until he breached my entrance and worked about an inch of his cock inside me. I expected him to bottom out on the first pass and was ready for it, but he surprised me once again.

Instead of one deep thrust, Dex used fast mini strokes to move in a little bit at a time. It was amazing—but fucking frustrating at the same time. I wanted to feel all of him, and this was another fucking tease.

With a grunt of defiance, I pushed back, forcing him all the way inside me.

"Greedy little slut, aren't you?" Dex grabbed my hips and held me still. "You want me to fuck you?"

"Ugh!" I couldn't talk with the damn gag still in my mouth, but it was clearly a yes.

Crack. Crack. Crack. Crack. Crack.

Five spanks timed with the first five strokes of his cock were enough to send me right back to my happy place, and my entire body relaxed as Dex fucked me harder than I'd ever gotten it before.

He dragged my hips back as he slammed forward, and the sounds of our impacting skin echoed in the room like cracks of thunder.

I was so lost in pleasure I couldn't keep up with what was happening. He was fucking me while randomly spanking me, reaching around to stroke my dick, and pulling on my hair. Every nerve in my body was alive and sparking with electricity. Everything felt amazing, but it was right on the edge of being too much and hurting.

I lost track of time as I slipped deeper and deeper into the pleasure that was consuming me, and when I finally reached that blissful place, the moment right before orgasm, there was no denial—Dex kept on fucking and teasing me.

I came hard. My muscles contracted and released at a dizzying rate as pleasure poured through me. I screamed and cried out around my gag, and when the first aftershock hit, I almost collapsed.

"Fuck, I'm close." Dex pulled out of me, the abrupt exit leaving me feeling empty. I heard the snap of latex. Was he going to creampie me?

Dex appeared in front of me, kneeling on either side of my arms as I held myself up. His cock was thick and flushed, and rock-fucking-hard. His hands fumbled as they undid the gag, and when it was off and tossed away, I opened my mouth as wide as I could, inviting him to fuck it.

"Yes, that's it." Dex grabbed a fistful of my hair with one hand and guided his cock between my lips with the other. He was slick with precum, and I groaned in pure pleasure when the slightly sweet, slightly tangy flavor coated my tongue.

"Take this fucking dick. Choke on it."

He didn't have to tell me twice. I relaxed my throat and let him go to town. He wasn't being gentle, and I didn't want him to be. I'd always had a decent gag reflex, but every thrust Dex made was testing it.

My eyes watered as I fought through the face fucking. I was choking on it like he wanted, but so help me God, I was loving it.

"Fuck!"

Dex pulled his cock back just far enough that he could shoot his load into the back of my throat. I gagged and struggled as he milked every drop out of his weeping dick. Trying to breathe and swallow and not choke took all of my concentration, but before I could finish, Dex was pulling me up by my hair. His lips covered mine, and his tongue swept into my mouth, playing with the last of his cum before I swallowed it.

Now that was fucking hot. I loved to watch cum play in porn but never thought I'd find a guy who would do it with me.

Dex continued to kiss me as I swallowed the last of his load and pulled me so I was on my knees in front of him, our bodies mirroring each other. He broke the kiss just long enough to pull my still-bound arms up between us and then looped them over his head so I could hold onto him.

I was grateful for the move. My head was spinning, my body was tingling, and my muscles didn't feel as though they were under my control anymore. I clung to him a little more tightly than I would ever admit to, and his warm arms circled my body and held me just as tightly.

The kiss naturally slowed until we were just nipping at each other's lips. Dex gave me one last nip then shifted me so my head was on his shoulder.

"How do you feel?" he asked.

I was feeling more in control, but that was a complicated question with everything going on in my mind and body at that moment.

"Drained. Amazing. Satisfied. Exhausted...."

"Yeah, it was pretty good."

"Good? It was way better than good." I pulled back and looked into Dex's amazing blue eyes. "Try again."

"Is fan-fucking-tastic okay?"

"I'll accept it."

"Sorry, my brain is a little blood starved after that." He grinned cheekily. "Do you have any idea how perfect your ass is? It took every trick I have to not nut after about four seconds."

"You're going to have to teach me those tricks." I pulled my arms from around him and sat back on my heels. As fun as being cuffed was in the moment, I wanted to be free now that it was over.

"And why would I give away my secrets?" Dex slid off the bed and got the key to the handcuffs.

"So I can fuck you until your eyes roll back and you're begging me to end it because it's too good."

Dex paused after undoing the first cuff and looked up at me, something primal and hungry flashing in his eyes.

"You think you could make me tap out? I thought you wanted it vanilla when you fuck me?"

"Vanilla, yes. Boring, no." I rubbed the skin of my wrists when he pulled the second cuff free. "I want you begging and pleading and screaming for me."

"I'm all for that. We'll have to get something easier on your skin. You fight them too much." Dex nodded to my wrists, and I glanced down. Two red circles were clearly visible.

"That's not obvious or anything." I twisted my wrists around to check out the extent of the marks. "Oh, well. We can alternate between leather and the cuffs. I like them too much to give them up."

"What about the evidence?"

"Fuck it. I'm going to be bruised to shit under my clothes, I might as well have something I can look at to remember."

"Oh, trust me." Dex pulled me onto the bed with him and drew me up against his chest. "You're not going to need marks to remember."

"No?"

"No."

"If you say so." I shrugged playfully and looked up at him.

"I say so."

"Yes, sir," I said teasingly, but the second the word was out of my mouth, it felt wrong. "Yes, daddy," I corrected.

I didn't give a fuck if Dex wasn't the traditional definition of a daddy. The way he owned and dominated me was more than enough to make that word work in my mind, and it felt right.

Dex grinned, his eyes alight with pleasure and something darker that I couldn't quite place. "That's my good boy."

His tone sent a shiver through my body, and I snuggled up to him. There was no doubt in my mind that Dex had only shown me a piece of what he had to offer, and I couldn't wait to see the rest.

www.ingramcontent.com/pod-product-compliance
Lightning Source LLC
Chambersburg PA
CBHW051718050726
47598CB00003B/950